Puss in Boots

Adapted by Rob M. Worley
Illustrated by Mike Dubisch

WAYLAND

First published in 2014 by Wayland

Copyright © 2014 Wayland

Wayland
338 Euston Road
London NW1 3BH

Wayland Australia
Level 17/207 Kent Street
Sydney, NSW 2000

Adapted Text by Rob M. Worley
Illustrations by Mike Dubisch
Colours by Wes Hartman
Edited by Stephanie Hedlund
Interior Layout by Kristen Fitzner Denton and Alyssa Peacock
Book Design and Packaging by Shannon Eric Denton
Cover Design by Alyssa Peacock

Copyright © 2008 by Abdo Consulting Group

A cataloguing record for this title is available at the British Library.
Dewey number: 823.9'2

Printed in China

ISBN: 978 0 7502 7828 7

Wayland is a division of Hachette Children's Books, an Hachette UK company.
www.hachette.co.uk

There was once a farmer who had three sons. He had only three things to leave to his sons:

The oldest son took the corn field.

The middle son took the donkey.

All that was left for the youngest son was his father's favourite cat.

Young Carabas didn't know what to do with the cat.

'My brothers can use the field and the donkey to earn a good living' said Carabas. 'But what good is this cat?'

'Cheer up, my good master' the cat said to him.
'I can do plenty. All I need is a bag and a pair
of boots.'

Carabas had seen how clever the cat was at chasing
mice. Perhaps he could do plenty with a good pair
of boots.

Puss set out with his new boots on.

He laid his bag filled with lettuce on the ground.

Soon a rabbit hopped in to eat the lettuce.

Puss closed the bag and trapped the rabbit.

Puss took the rabbit to the palace.

'Here is a gift from Prince Carabas' the cat said.
Carabas wasn't really a prince. But Puss was happy
to say it anyway.

The gift pleased the king.

Day after day the cat brought gifts to the king.

One day the king said 'I would like to meet Prince Carabas.'

The cat drew a map to his master's castle. Carabas didn't live in a castle. But Puss was happy to draw it anyway.

Carabas did not know what Puss had been doing.

'I gave you your boots, but you've done nothing' moaned Carabas.

'Trust me, good master' Puss said. 'If you do as I say now, things will start looking up.'

'First you must take a bath' said the cat.

'But I took a bath last month' moaned Carabas.

'Do as I say, good master' Puss said. 'Take off your clothes. I will guard them.'

But Puss did not guard the clothes.

He hid them under a large stone.

At that very moment, the king passed by.

'Help! Help! Prince Carabas is drowning!' shouted Puss.

The king stopped.

'Save dear Prince Carabas' the king ordered his men.

'Thieves! Thieves stole my master's fine clothes!' shouted Puss.

'There, there' the king said. 'Don't worry. We have extra clothes for your master.'

Carabas felt much better with a bath and new clothes. The cat was right! Things were looking up!

'Prince Carabas, I'd like you to meet my daughter' said the king.

Carabas thought the princess was beautiful.

Carabas joined the king and the princess.

'I'll keep the road clear of thieves' said Puss.

He ran ahead.

Puss met some workers in a field.

'When the king comes by, tell him you work for Prince Carabas' Puss told them.

'But this is not his field' said one worker.

'Do as I say or you shall be chopped up into mincemeat' said Puss.

Later the king passed.

'Whose field do you harvest?' the king asked.

'It belongs to Prince Carabas' said the frightened worker.

'This is my best field,' Carabas said.

Ahead, Puss found more workers.

They were not afraid of him. So the cat used his claw to cut the boss's belt.

'Do as I say or you'll all lose your trousers!' Puss shouted.

The king arrived moments later.

'Whose apples are these?' asked the king.

'They belong to Prince Carabas' replied the worker.

Up ahead, Puss came to a large castle.

The castle belonged to the richest and most terrible ogre the land had ever known.

'Are you afraid of me?' the ogre asked.

'Of course' said Puss. 'A cat is no match for an ogre.'

'This is true' laughed the ogre.

'I have heard you have great powers' said Puss.
'That you can change into any kind of creature.
But I don't believe it.'

'I will prove it to you' replied the ogre.

The ogre changed into a huge lion. He roared a
lion's roar.

Puss was so scared he jumped out of his boots!

'Are you afraid of me?' the ogre asked again.

'Yes' said Puss. 'A cat is no match for a lion.'

The ogre changed back to normal.

'There is no creature I cannot change into' the ogre said.

'I doubt you could become a tiny creature like a mouse' Puss said.

'I'll show you!' shouted the ogre.

So the ogre changed himself into a mouse.

This time Puss was not afraid. A mouse is no match for a cat.

Moments later, the king arrived.

'Welcome to the palace of Prince Carabas'
said Puss.

'I had no idea you were so rich' the king said.

'Neither did I!' Carabas said.

There was a huge meal waiting in the castle dining room.

'Master has prepared a feast' said Puss.

This food was meant for the ogre. But Puss was happy to share it anyway.

28

Everyone enjoyed the great meal.

For the first time, Carabas felt happy.

This young prince had charmed the princess
and her father.

Carabas asked the king if he could marry
the princess.

They were wed that same day.

Puss became a great lord.

He never chased mice again, for he had already done plenty of that.